THE BLACK ATHLETE™
Volume 2

By John D. White

San Marcos California 2022

The Black Athlete Volume 2

Written by: John D. White

Published by: Destined For Greatness Creative Writing & Publishing, a branch of DFG Creative Expressions L.L.C. San Marcos, California 2022

Published in the United States of America

Epigraph

This literary work was written to inspire black and brown girls around the world! To inspire them to know that it's okay to speak up, and be confident in their God-given abilities, and to walk in their divine purpose unapologetically. This book will give them the courage to weather the storms and challenges that life will throw at them, and one day help others to do the same.

Dedication

The Black Athlete Volume 2 is dedicated to ALL the Black and Brown Girls across the world!

To the Black Girl that's striving to be ALL she can be! To the Black Girl that's struggling privately and seeking an outlet to be free! To the Black Girl that knows NO LIMITS in life and believes that ANYTHING is possible! I LOVE YOU Black Girl!

Keep PUSHING, keep STRIVING, keep BELIEVING, because the WORLD is yours for the taking!

John D. White

The Author at A Glance

A native of Detroit, MI, John D. White has a passion to uplift and move forward the culture through his literary and philanthropy work through his Non-Profit organization, The J.D. White P.L.A.Y. Foundation. The Black Athlete Brand has transcended the black community in a monumental way and has inspired many Black Athlete's across the globe to take pride in WHO and WHAT they are... POWERFUL beyond measure.

The father of 2 beautiful sons (Israel & Josiah), White's impact in the Detroit community has changed the life of many inner-city youth for the greater. "Just A Kid... Trying to Make It" is The Black Athlete motto known across the world. "To invoke change, is to first be the change you want to see..." That's the saying that John D. White lives by and continues to instill in today's youth.

John wrote The Black Athlete Volume 2, for it to give many young Black girls the courage to endure heartache, speak up, and walk in their God given destiny.

Acknowledgments

My Lord and Savior Jesus Christ… Where would I be if it wasn't for your grace and mercy? Thank you!

To my family, thank you for your endless support and belief in my vision as a writer and story-teller.

Israel & Josiah… You two are my "Why", the reason I push to be the best at whatever I do! I love you two FOR LIFE! You inspire me daily to be better at life, and I pray the blessings of the Lord upon your lives. Daddy loves you!

My Key… Let's make it last forever! Thank you for being YOU! I LOVE YOU!

Bishop Will Thornton & the King of Kings International Church family. Words can't describe my gratitude and love for you all. My life has been nothing but BLESSED since God planted me in the ministry. Thank you!!

To my friends, thank you for being there and supporting me in all that I have put my mind to do. You know who you are!

To J Scales Protégé! Your gift is second to none, and it's going to take you before GREAT men! Thank you for allowing me to introduce you to the world!

Blessings on Blessings!

Warning—Disclaimer

Introduction

Bianca became numb, and her body had seemed to become frozen. She sat in disbelief that R.J. had died in her arms. Even though the paramedics continued to perform CPR on his lifeless body, she knew he was gone. Bianca's mind raced, yet her body was motionless, then came anxiety, and her very own breath felt like it was leaving her. "Oh my God," she thought. "I have to call Mr. and Mrs. Watkins." She didn't know how or what she would say to them, so she broke down and wept deeply.

"Young lady, may I have a few words with you?" asked the homicide detective.

Visibly disturbed and shaken up, Bianca softly answered, "Yes Sir." As those words came out of her mouth during all the commotion, a loud scream rung out. "GOD NO, NO, NO, NO! Not my baby..." The tears flowed, as Honey (R.J.'s mother) fell to her knees while clutching her stomach. Ray stood there in disbelief, as he recognized the gym shoes on his son's feet that stuck out from the tarp that covered his lifeless body. Ray and Honey heard about the shooting on the news, so they tried countless times to contact R.J.'s cellphone, but they couldn't reach him, so they rushed to the scene to see if it was truly R.J.

Ray never cried, he just stood in silence while looking down at his only child covered by a black tarp that read DPD Homicide.

"Mr. and Mrs. Watkins," said Bianca with a trembling voice, and a face covered with tears. As they turned around, they both immediately grabbed Bianca and hugged her.

"Are you all the parents?" asked the officer. Ray looked up and said, "Yes, I'm Ray Watkins, and this is my wife Honey."

Knowing who R.J. was, the officer sadly said, "I'm sorry for your loss, my name is Officer Maurice Cox, and I'll be the lead detective on this case. If you don't mind, I would like for you all to come down to the 5th Precinct, so we can ask you a few questions."

Taking a deep breath, and one more glance down at R.J.'s body, Ray gently said, "Sure that is fine..."

While at the police station, Detective Cox questioned Bianca about the incident, and while she described the shooter, Ray shouted out, "J.J.?! You mean to tell me that J.J. killed my son?!" With a perplexed look on her face, Honey said, "How is that possible? I thought he was locked up for killing Sammy!"

Bianca sat and cried... It felt as if part of her died in front of that Coney Island restaurant. Detective Cox vowed that he would catch J.J., and that he will put him away for good. Sadly, another senseless crime had claimed the life of one of Detroit's beloved sons.

Detective Cox gave them one of his cards and told them to keep in touch with him, and if anything, else comes up, to give him a call.

Volume 2

Chapter 1

15 years later...

It's a hot summer day at Peterson park on the westside. The four basketball courts were full as the D.J.'s music blast throughout the neighborhood, and the smell of barbeque filled the air.

"Who got next?" asked Tom-Tom, known as the neighborhood hoop legend. Looking around, nobody spoke up to claim the next game, so Tom-Tom said, "Well, I guess it's me!"

As Tom-Tom was speaking, running across the grass to the basketball courts was this curly haired girl, as she got to the court, she said, "Game still not over?! How long does it take a team to score 10 points?"

Laughing as he looked at the young lady, Tom-Tom said, "Little lady, what's your name?" Looking up at Tom-Tom that stood at 6 ft 8 inches tall, she replied, "My name is Ce-Ce..., Yours?"

13, soon to be 14 year-old Cecilia Adams was probably one of the most talented female basketball players you'll ever see. Nobody knew much about her, other than she'll pop up every now and again at the basketball court.

With an amazed smirk on his face, he replied, "My name is Tom-Tom... So, I guess you're playing right?" As Ce-Ce was bending over to lace her shoes she exhaled, looked up at Tom-Tom and said, "Of-course I'm playing, that's the only reason I'm here. It's my next... You good though, you can run with me."

The look on Tom-Tom's face said it all, he thought to himself, "Who is this little girl, and where did she come from?"

Game point!! Yelled out someone standing on the side watching the game. Everyone in the park had gathered around to watch this little girl embarrass everyone that stepped on the court. Tom-Tom was in total shock at the way Ce-Ce could play basketball, and how she did it with confidence, swag, and attitude.

 As Ce-Ce dribbled the ball, she made sound effects with her mouth. "Pop-pop... Pop-pop-pop," followed with a "Got em', as she made the game winning shot, and made everyone go crazy!

"Yo, how did you learn to play ball like that? You just don't wake up doing the stuff you did, it's either in your blood, or the basketball Gods smiled down on you!" said Tom-Tom with a look of disbelief on his face.

Shrugging her shoulders, Ce-Ce said, "I don't know... I get asked that all the time... I just play, it's kind of weird... I can't explain it."

While grabbing her cellphone and water off the bench, Ce-Ce said, "Aight everybody, I'll catch y'all next time," as she ran off to hurry home.

Na-Na's House

"Ce-Ce is that you?" said Mrs. Velma as she heard someone come in the front door.

Mrs. Velma was known in the neighborhood as Na-Na because all the kids seen her as an Auntie to everyone. Na-Na was a gentle soul, and her white

hair glowed even though she was just in her mid-50's, but her wisdom excelled them all.

"Hey Na-Na, yes it's me. I'm about to shower and get dressed, so I can hurry and get back before curfew."

Ce-Ce was a ward of the state, and she lived in an all-girls facility downtown Detroit called the Covenant Center for Girls, better known as CCG. Ce-Ce never knew her parents, when she was born her mother left her at the hospital to be put up for adoption. Na-Na was in the process of trying to adopt Ce-Ce, so every weekend with the permission of CCG she would come stay at Na-Na's house.

"Yes, hurry and get cleaned up... Child you smell like outside, so I know you've been down at the park playing basketball. Did you give them the flux again?" asked Na-Na with a slight chuckle.

"I tried to Na-Na!" yelled Ce-Ce from the bathroom.
"Child, they be talking about you in the neighborhood, trying to figure out who you are, and where you come from," said Na-Na.

Drying her hair with a towel as she got out of the shower, Ce-Ce said, "You know Na-Na... Some guy asked me that today. He asked me where I learnt how to play basketball, and where did I come from. Crazy thing is, I didn't know how to answer him."

Looking at Ce-Ce, Na-Na replied, "Sweety, you were sent from heaven, and that's all you and anyone else need to know. Keep being you, and don't apologize to anyone for the gift that God gave you! Now hurry up so we can get going." With a huge smile on her face, Ce-Ce said, "Yes Ma'am."

Chapter 2

On the 30 minute drive to take Ce-Ce back to the facility, her and Na-Na spoke about life, and what it would be like if her parents were in her life.

That always haunted Ce-Ce, and she battled with depression from wondering why her parents didn't want her. At times Na-Na would just allow Ce-Ce to vent to her, because she truly didn't understand her pain. It broke her heart to see such a beautiful young lady feel like she's worthless and was left because her parents didn't want her.

Reaching her hand over to Ce-Ce to embrace her hand, Na-Na said, "Baby, God knows everything, from the birds to the bees and why they sing... We will never understand everything God does, but we have to know that it's working out for our good Ce-Ce." As they held hands, Ce-Ce turned to the window and wept.

"Back to the Cottage"

"Ok lights out ladies! You all know what time it is!" yelled the Youth Specialist Toni Jones, who the girls called Mr. T.J.

Mr. T.J. was an opposing figure that stood at 6 foot 3 inches tall, and he weighed a solid 245 lbs. He was often compared to a dark skinned Suge Knight, because of his bald head and full beard. He always wore dark shades, even if it was inside a building, it was a way he can hide where and who he was looking at. The girls really didn't like him, they viewed him as a "creep," and a few accusations were brought against him for sexual misconduct, but for some reason they always got swept under the rug.

As Ce-Ce walked into the building, she was still visibly disturbed from the conversation she had in the car with Na-Na.

You're pushing it Cecilia! I understand you were on a home visit, but there's still rules and regulations you have to follow, like being back here on time!" said Mr. T.J. in a very smug and sarcastic way.

With her head down and walking to her room, Ce-Ce softly said, "Yea, I know. It won't happen again." She closed her room door, set her bags down, and just laid on the bed looking up at the ceiling in deep thought until she fell asleep.

As the girls woke up the next morning, they all took turns taking showers because in their housing unit, there was only one bathroom for 8 girls. The housing unit or "cottage" as they called it was named Hawthorne, and the cottages were separated by ages.

The Hawthorne 8

Within Hawthorne you have **Ce-Ce** who is the outspoken leader, but at the same time she is quiet and very observant, some call her the "Quiet Storm." Then there's Chanelle a young Mexican/American girl, who everyone calls *Nelly*. She is always up for a fight, and most of the time looking for one. Nelly was sexually abused multiple times by her uncle while living with her grandmother, whom she went to live with after her mother died in a house fire that she (Nelly) started. She ended up at CCG after she was involved in a bowling alley brawl, that caused several people to be hospitalized.

Then there is **Sarah**, a shy white girl from the suburbs who read books and journal all day, but she pretty much keeps to herself. She lost both of her parents in a car accident when she was 3, and bounced around from foster home to foster home, until she landed at CCG 2 years ago.

Then there is **Taylor**, she's often made fun of by her peers because of her weight and hygiene issues. However, her sense of humor is second to none! She's always the life of the party, and the funniest person at CCG. She tries to mask her pain by keeping everyone laughing, and she does a good job at it. Her mother dropped her off at daycare one day, and never came back to get her. She eventually went to live with her aunt, and while there she was repeatedly molested by a family friend.

RaNelle is the typical "girlie" girl that you wouldn't assume will be in a placement like CCG. Everyone call's her Ra-Ra, but if you're not careful she'll steal the shirt right off your back. Part of the judge's order was for Ra-Ra to serve 6 months at CCG and 2 years of probation, for a shoplifting spree her and a group of friends went on, that lasted over the span of 2 months before they were caught.

Then there's the twins **Heaven** and **Nevaeh**, better known as "Thunder and Lightning." These two always keep confusion going on within the cottage! They were born and raised on the eastside of Detroit and came to CCG when CPS (Child Protection Services) was alerted to their home because drugs were being sold out of it. There were no family members willing to take them in, so the judge ordered them to a placement.

Lastly, there's Lindsay, who's known as **Zae'**. She's as bougie, sassy, and mean as they come. None of the other girls in the cottage care for her, and they often stay away from her. Nobody really know why she's at CCG, because her father is a rich chemical engineer that works for a large corporation. The rumor is that Zae' struggled with drug and alcohol abuse, and it led to her stealing to support her habit because her father stopped giving her money.

Breakfast Time

"Ok ladies, it's time for breakfast...," said the A.M. Youth Specialist Ms. Adriana. The girls loved Ms. Adriana, she was young, and she could relate to the girls in a way that a lot of the staff couldn't.

"Ms. Adriana, it smells like something is burning in the kitchen, you sure you know what you're doing?" said Taylor jokingly.

Shaking her head as she put the plates on the table, Ms. Adriana said, "It's too early in the morning for jokes Taylor, just make sure your hygiene is done before you sit down at this table."

As the girls gathered around to take their seats at the table, Ms. Adriana noticed someone was missing... "Ok, it's only seven girls at the table, who's missing?" Almost at the same time everyone said, "Ce-Ce!"

With a slight chuckle, Taylor said, "You know Ce-Ce is ALWAYS the last one to the table every morning, I don't even know why you asked who's missing."

Nodding her head in agreement, Nelly said, "Facts!"
"You know I can hear y'all talking about me, right?" said Ce-Ce as she sat down at the table.

Smacking her lips and rolling her eyes at the same time, Nelly said, "Girl, nobody cares if you heard them or not, the truth is the truth... YOU. ARE. ALWAYS. LATE. Periodt."

".... Not today Nelly, because I **PROMISE** you, it's not gonna go well for you, so just miss me with the smart remarks," said Ce-Ce.

Stepping in to defuse any tension that was about to happen, Ms. Adriana said, "Ok, who's going to bless the food this morning? Don't everybody speak at once."

The girls looked around to see who would bless the food, and finally Sarah yelled out, "Forget it, I'll do it!"

Chapter 3

As the day went on, the girls completed their chores and relaxed until it was time for their Girl Talks group session. It gave the girls a time and a safe place to express their feelings, and to talk about anything that's weighing them down.

The Girl Talk sessions were usually ran by Ms. Susie, who was part of the afternoon staff. Ms. Susie started working at CCG to keep herself busy after she retired from being a schoolteacher for 35 years. She always wanted to give back to young ladies, so it was the ideal job for her.

"Ok everyone, time to gather around so we can start our group session for this evening... How is everyone doing today?" asked Ms. Susie. Silence was the response she received, but most of the girls shrugged their shoulders, as if to say they're ok...

"Ok, well I'll assume everyone is doing ok then... So, who wants to be the first to speak tonight? Ladies remember, this is a safe space for you to express yourself and speak your mind. This is a non-judgement zone here.

"I'll go first!" shouted out Heaven...

Shocked by her enthusiasm, Ms. Susie said, "Well go ahead Heaven, what is it that you want to say?"

Heaven sat there as if she was off in a deep thought, or trying to gather her words, then Heaven said, "You know... It's hard being here, because every day that I am here, it reminds me of the reason I'm here... Does that make sense?" Everyone shook their heads as if to say "Yes."

Heaven went on to say, "How is it that nobody in my family wanted us?! How could they turn their backs on us?! Me and my sister didn't ask to be in that situation! We didn't even ask to be born, let alone born into that lifestyle!"

Seeing how emotional her sister was, Nevaeh ran over to comfort her... "It's ok sissy..., I promise you we're gonna be ok, I promise!" said Nevaeh.

Everyone sat in silence as Nevaeh consoled Heaven, the energy in the room shifted as everyone's mind turned with thoughts of their own situations.

"Well, I cry myself to sleep most nights..." said a soft spoken Sarah. She continued, "Imagine feeling cheated by God, and always wondering why me? Why my parents? Why did they have to die like that in a car crash, right after they dropped me off to my grandma's house... Why couldn't I have died with them? Why leave me alone in this world to have to find my own way, and deal with this pain and hurt? WHY ME?!! I always hear people say, "Don't ask God why," but who else has the answers? It was His decision to take my Mom and Dad away!! It's just not fair."

"Imagine having your parents there..., but you still feel invisible as if you don't even exist. Then one day you decide to go into your Mother's medicine cabinet and take one of her prescribed pills, just to see how it'll make you feel, since she said they were for pain. I figured maybe it'll heal or take away the pain I was feeling."

Everyone was stuck, and somewhat in a shock that Zae was speaking. She continued, "Yes my dad is rich, and yes I don't want or need for any of the superficial things that people believe will make them happy. All I ever wanted was to be loved, or even acknowledged from time to time. I started burying myself in my dad's alcohol, I felt free, I felt at ease, I didn't have a worry in the world. I began finding older people that would buy me drugs and alcohol, and things spent out of control fast."

The girls spoke freely about how they were feeling on the inside, and Ms. Susie listened to every word they spoke. When the session was over, she encouraged each of them, and gave them some words to help carry them through...

"Ladies, there's always going to be test and trails in life, we just have to figure out how to get through them. Each one of you have dealt with some unthinkable and for the most part, some unbearable situations in your short-young- lives. I hate to sound cliché or like a broken record, but God is working it all out for your good, He know you and He sees the pain you're feeling, so be encouraged and don't give up..."

"Ahhh-Ha-ha-ha-ha...!" A burst of laughter from Taylor broke the silence in the room, and while shaking her head as she continued to laugh, Taylor said, "Ms. Susie, you preached a whole sermon up in here! No disrespect, but did you hear ANYTHING that any of us said tonight?! It's hard to hear what

God is going to do, when all we can go by is what He has allowed to happen to us, and to OUR families!"

The way that Taylor felt was how all the girls felt at that very moment, even though they knew that Ms. Susie didn't mean to offend anyone, it was just the way they felt.

"Honestly, I'm the only one in here because of something that I did to myself," said Ra-Ra. "I chose to steal and make stupid decisions. My parents had nothing to do with that, and I feel everyone's pain, trust me I do. Y'all don't get mad at Ms. Susie for trying to help and make us feel better, because we're all gonna be here until we age out, get adopted, or hopefully for me go back home. That's our reality for now."

As emotions ran high, and the tears rolled down some of the young ladies faces, for the first time Ms. Susie felt helpless and at a loss for words. However, she found the courage to try to say something to ease the tension in the room.

"Ladies, I'm sorry. I'm sorry if I offended anyone, and I'm sorry if I made you feel like what you're going through is not real. All I can do is pray for better days, even though most of you can't see them. I love you all, and I will always be here for the Hawthorne 8."

As Ce-Ce jumped up to give Ms. Susie a hug, she said, "Ahhh I love you SO much Ms. Susie!" All the girls followed her lead to hug and tell Ms. Susie they loved her as well.

Chapter 4

The Girls Talk session had the girls drained emotionally and physically. They laughed, they cried, they got angry, and they became sad. It's easy to say that their emotions were all over the place.

As Mr. T.J. came in to take over the night shift, Nelly said, "Ms. Susie, you sure you can't stay tonight, and send Mr. T.J. back home? Dude trips, and we ain't got time for that tonight..."

Standing at the desk looking down at some paperwork, Mr. T.J. said, "You do know that I'm standing right here, and I can hear you... Right?"
In typical Nelly fashion, she responded, "Ummm you do know that I don't care... Right?"

She rolled her eyes and said, "Good night Ms. Susie, I'll see you tomorrow," and she walked to her room.

Shaking his head, Mr. T.J. said to Ms. Susie, "That girl is going to have a hard life if she doesn't get her attitude together."

With frustration in her voice, Ms. Susie looked at Mr. T.J. and said, "You must learn to love the girls where they're at, and not where you want them to be. If you truly were transparent, and took the time to get to know them, maybe you'll handle them with a little more grace. Learn to speak life into them, instead of saying there's no hope for them."

Shocked by what Ms. Susie said to him, Mr. T.J. responded, "Ms. Susie, I'm very transparent, but I'm also a realest when it comes to the obvious. Her attitude is terrible, and everyone knows that about Nelly. She needs to get it together, that's all I'm saying."

Looking back down at the papers, Mr. T.J. notices that Ce-Ce has a court appearance she's supposed to be at tomorrow.

"Do Ce-Ce know she's supposed to be in court tomorrow about her adoption hearing?"

Nodding her head as she grabs her bags from under the table, Ms. Susie said, "Yes, she knows about it, and she's nervous as well. I believe she really likes Ms. Velma, so I hope it all works out."

As Ms. Susie walked out of the cottage she said, "Well Mr. T.J., you enjoy your night Sir, and we'll see each other tomorrow."

"Ladies, it's about that time to shower and turn the lights out for the night. Ce-Ce you have to be up early in the morning because you have a court date, so you may want to go first so you can get some rest," said Mr. T.J.

Ce-Ce was in her room undressing because she had already decided to shower first so she could get to bed. While in her room, she couldn't hear Mr. T.J. talking to her because she had her air pods in her ears listening to music.

Mr. T.J. yelled, "Ce-Ce you hear me talking to you?!"

Mr. T.J. became irritated because he didn't get a response from Ce-Ce, so he grabbed his keys from around his neck as they dangled from his key chain and unlocked the door to walk in without first knocking. As he opened the door and looked up, there stood Ce-Ce naked and embarrassed as her and Mr. T.J. locked eyes, his eyes panned down her body, and she instantly felt violated!

As she grabbed for a towel to cover her nakedness, at the same time snatching the air pods out of her ears, Ce-Ce shouted, "Mr. T.J. what are you doing?!!! **GET THE F%^& OUT OF MY ROOM!!**"

Hearing the commotion coming from Ce-Ce's room, the girls came running to see what was going on.

"Ce-Ce are you ok? What's going on?" asked Nevaeh.

Trembling and visibly upset Ce-Ce said, "I'm in here getting ready to get in the shower, and while completely naked, Mr. T.J. burst into my room!"

With a look of shock on all their faces, Taylor says, "See, that nigga is a pervert! I told y'all! You need to report him Ce-Ce, this ain't the first time he pulled some mess like this!"

All the girls stood in silence, while Mr. T.J. went back to his desk to begin filling out an incident report.

Looking at Mr. T.J., Nelly said, "Nah nigga, don't be trying to fill out an incident report! Did you apologize to her? Why do you think you can just burst in our rooms like that anyway? I hope your perverted a## burn in hell! It's nigga's like you we're trying to stay away from!"

Standing up from his chair, Mr. T.J. yelled, "Nelly!! Go to your room NOW! Everybody in their rooms! I'll call you out one by one to shower, and Ce-Ce you go first!

"Yelling out of her room, Ce-Ce screamed, "Go to HELL Mr. T.J.!"

Unexpected Visitor

Knock, knock, knock.... "Babe, can you get the door?!" yelled Honey from the top of the stairs.

Taking a deep breath as he got up off the sofa, Ray made his way to the door to open it. As he opened the door, he stood there in amazement as if he was shocked to see who was on the other side of the door.

"Hi Mr. Watkins, how have you been? Do you mind if I come in?" asked Bianca.

Struggling to get his words out, Ray said, "Um sure... forgive me, please come in Bianca."

Walking towards the stairs, Ray yelled for Honey to come down. "Honey come see who's here! You won't believe who stopped by to see us."

Getting off the treadmill, Honey grabbed a towel to wipe the sweat off her face. As she walked down the stairs, she wondered who it could be that stopped by their home to see them. "Oh My God! Bianca, is that you sweetie? Come here and give me a hug!" said Honey with excitement.

They cried, hugged, and laughed all at the same time, as they became overwhelmed with emotions.

"Bianca, we're just happy and surprised to see you... We haven't seen you in years. How have you been? Is everything ok?" asked Ray.

As Bianca stood there still holding Honey's hand, she asked them if they could sit down.

"Sure, let's go in the family room, we can sit in there," said Honey. Ray sat in the recliner, while Bianca and Honey sat on the love seat.

"Forgive me Bianca, can I get you anything to drink?" asked Honey. Bianca politely declined. "So, tell us what have you been up to, and what brings you here? It's been what... 14 or 15 years since we last seen you?" said Honey.

With an embarrassed and shameful look on her face, Bianca said, "Yes, it's been that long. I had to get away after everything happened with RJ..., and just for my mental state. However, that's why I'm here today... There's something I need to tell you guys, that I probably should've told you years ago..."

Chapter 5

As Ce-Ce sat up in her bed, she couldn't help but think about what the outcome would be in court. She became overwhelmed with anxiety, got out of the bed, and started pacing back and forth in the room.

While Ce-Ce paced the floor, there was a knock at her room door. It was Ms. Adriana.

"Good morning Ce-Ce... I was just making sure you were up. We're going to get ready to leave soon, so shower and get dressed, so you can get something to eat before we head out."

Nodding her head, an overwhelmed Ce-Ce said, "Yes Ma'am, I'll be out soon."

The Nervous Ride

"Ok Ce-Ce... It's time to go sweetie," said Ms. Adriana as she grabbed the car keys out of the file cabinet.

While on the ride to court, Ms. Adriana noticed that Ce-Ce was nervous, so as she looked at her through the rear-view mirror, she said, "Are you ok Ce-Ce? How are you feeling... You look a little worried back there."

"I can't lie Ms. Adriana, I'm nervous... It's hard walking into a situation knowing you don't have any control over it. I really like Na-Na, and I want to live with her, so I hope the judge feels the same way, you know...?" said Ce-Ce.

"It's all going to work out Ce-Ce, I truly believe that." said Ms. Adriana

The Confession

As Bianca sat next to Honey, she rubbed her hands together nervously as she prepared to speak...

With a look of concern on her face, Honey said, "Is everything ok Bianca? Don't be afraid to speak to us sweetie."

Taking another deep breath, Bianca said, "Mr. and Mrs. Watkins, this has been eating me up for years and I wish things could've been different, but with everything that was happening with R.J. being killed, I became overwhelmed and scared... I was young and I didn't know what to do..."

"Bianca, just tell us what's going on... It's ok," said Ray.

Nodding her head, Bianca said, "Ok... Me and R.J. had sex while up at school, and I got pregnant... The day R.J. got killed we were coming to surprise you for your birthday Mrs. Watkins, and we were going to tell you all then... R.J. was terrified, because he didn't know how you all were going to take the news..."

Putting her head down, Bianca began to cry uncontrollably, while Honey and Ray sat in disbelief at what they just heard.

"Bianca... What happened to the baby? Ummm I'm just... Wow...," said Ray as if he was at a loss for words.

Honey went over to console Bianca, as she rubbed her back she said, "It's ok sweetie... Sit up, tell us what happened to the baby. Did you have an abortion?"

Wiping her face as the tears continued to flow, Bianca said, "No Ma'am..." Sitting up in his chair, Ray said, "Wait?! What are you saying? We have a grandchild, and we never knew?!"

Still crying, Bianca said, "I left her at the hospital to be put up for adoption... Nobody knew because I hid the pregnancy. I was so depressed after R.J. died, I left school and moved back in with my Grandmother... She had no idea that I was pregnant."

"So, it was a girl...? Did you name her?" asked Honey.

"Yes Ma'am... Cecilia... I named her Cecilia Danyell...," said Bianca." Ray sat in disbelief as he looked at the ceiling, while his thoughts raced through his head...

Chapter 6

Ce-Ce's Day in Court

As Ce-Ce sat nervously in the court room, her mind wondered what the outcome would be today in court.

Everyone was sitting in silence when the door from the Judge's chambers opened, and the Bailiff said, "All rise! As the Honorable Judge Mikki Stanton enters the courtroom."

Judge Stanton was known as a no nonsense type of judge, and many people left out of his courtroom disappointed. With him, everything had to make sense and be in the best interest of the child involved in the adoption process.

Judge Stanton was an opposing figure, he stood at 6 foot 7 inches tall and weighed nearly 300 pounds. He came up in the foster system and devoted his life to making sure children went to the best foster homes under his watch.

As Judge Stanton adjusted his glasses and mulled over the paperwork, he slowly looked up to find Ms. Velma.

Once he focused his eyes on Ms. Velma, Judge Stanton said, "Ma'am, can you please see me in my chambers?"

As Ms. Velma entered the chambers, Judge Stanton asked her to have a seat.

Sitting down in his chair, Judge Stanton removed his glasses and wiped his forehead...

"You may be wondering why I called you into my chambers Ma'am." Interrupting Judge Stanton, Ms. Velma said, "Ms. Velma, please call me Ms. Velma."

Acknowledging her request, Judge Stanton said, "Please forgive me Ms. Velma... Nevertheless, as I was saying... You're probably wondering why I called you in here. As I was looking over the paperwork, I recognized all the great things you have done in the community. I recognized your face from years ago, as I would go with my foster Mother and Father to volunteer at the nursing home on East Jefferson."

With a look of amazement on her face, Ms. Velma said, "Wow, those were some years ago when I used to go down on Jefferson to Willie B's Nursing Home. I sure do hate they tore it down; many lives were altered after that... Just sad."

"Yes Ma'am... I mean Ms. Velma, said Judge Stanton as he quickly corrected himself.

He went on to say, "I brought you into my chambers to personally thank you in private, and to let you know that I have seen your good works, and I used to watch you as you gave the residents ice cream, played checkers with them, and played the piano as they sang songs."

Ms. Velma began to cry...

"Don't cry Ms. Velma, I just pray that you make this young lady's life a joy as well... That you will teach her to appreciate humanity, and to treat others with love and kindness...," said Judge Stanton.

Ms. Velma's face lit up as those words came out of Judge Stanton's mouth, and she became overwhelmed with joy.

"Thank you so much your Honor, I promise you that I will do the best that I can with Ce-Ce to instill values in her.," said Ms. Velma.

Nodding his head in agreement, Judge Stanton said, "I have no doubt that you will Ms. Velma, and once again I thank you for all that you do."

The Decision

When Ms. Velma walked back into the courtroom, Ce-Ce can tell she had been crying. Not knowing what to think, Ce-Ce was expecting the worse.

Looking back at Ms. Velma, Ce-Ce didn't know what to think...

"All Rise....," said the Bailiff.

As Judge Stanton took his seat, he looked at Ce-Ce and said...
"Young lady, it's not often that young people are blessed to leave a situation or placement like CCF and find a stable and caring home with someone who's going to pour greatness into them. Now hear me Cecilia... One can give you the tools and even the instructions to be great in life, but it's up to

you to use them wisely. Ms. Velma is a world changer, and a lover of people. Her track record speaks for itself, and you should be grateful that the good Lord seen fit for you to be with her. Take this with you Cecilia... Only the discipline ones are free in life, if you're not discipline you are a slave to your moods, and you are a slave to your passions. Stay disciplined young lady, and you will go far in life."

Looking up at Judge Stanton, Ce-Ce softly said, "Yes Sir."

As Judge Stanton shuffled the paperwork and stacked it, he went on to say...

"With that being said, I hereby order that Cecilia be placed in the foster care of Ms. Velma effective immediately... Court is adjourned."

Ce-Ce was overcome with emotions, as she buried her head in her hands and cried tears of joy.

Ms. Velma jumped up in excitement, while she wept and clapped her hands to the judge's decision.

See You Later

The ride back to CCF was quiet and kind of melancholy, because there were mixed emotions about Ce-Ce leaving to go live with Ms. Velma.
"I'm sad but at the same time happy that you've found a home Ce-Ce", said Ms. Adriana to break the ice... She continued, "We always knew that this day would come; however, you still can't prepare for the reality of it. This isn't the place for any young lady to live... I'm going to miss you Ce-Ce."

Blushing as she smiled at Ms. Adriana, Ce-Ce said, "Aww Ms. A, I'm going to miss you and all the girls in Hawthorne as well... I'm kind of nervous about everything, but I'm excited at the same time. Do you think I'll be able to come back and visit? I hope all the girls find homes, or can go back home..."

"Well, that's always the goal and hope for the girls, but sometimes it doesn't work out that way," said Ms. Adriana.

As they pulled up to Hawthorne, Ce-Ce took a deep sigh as she prepared herself to go into the cottage for possibly the last time.

Looking over at Ce-Ce, Ms. Adriana said, "Don't worry Ce-Ce... You'll be fine. Just take some time to gather your thoughts and get your emotions together."

As Ce-Ce sat in the car and looked at the cottage, memories filled her head. Both good and bad. She couldn't believe that this day was finally here.

"I guess I'll go in and say my good-byes and start packing up my things...," said Ce-Ce while she sat in the car as if she was stuck to her seat.

Fanning herself with a piece of paper, Ms. Adriana said, "Come on Ce-Ce, let's get out of this hot car... You'll be fine, and the girls are going to be happy for you. Trust me!"

Final Good-Bye

"SURPRISE!!" Yelled the girls as Ce-Ce walked into the cottage.

Overcome with emotions, Ce-Ce laughed and cried as everyone gave each other one big group hug.

"Ahh guys, why you making me cry? It's already hard enough knowing that I'm leaving the "Crazy 8," said Ce-Ce while still laughing and crying.

Looking over at Ms. Adriana, Ce-Ce nodded her head as if to say thank you.

The girls sat around and talked for a while, then Ms. Adriana said, "Ok Ce-Ce, it's time to get your things packed up. Ms. Velma will be here in a couple of hours to pick you up."

"Come on Ce-Ce, we will help you get all of your things packed up. It's the least we can do," said Heaven.

With a huge smile on her face, Ce-Ce said, "Thank you so much... I'm really gonna miss y'all."

Chapter 7

"Whew, I didn't realize I had so much stuff inside that little room," said Ce-Ce as she packed her last bag into Ms. Velma's mini-van.

All the girls stood outside and watched as Ce-Ce put the finishing touch on situating her bags.

Looking over at the girls, Ce-Ce said, "Well don't just stand there, come give me a hug good-bye!"

As they hugged, they cried tears of happiness as well as sadness because Ce-Ce was leaving for good.

"Why are you girls making me cry...," Said Ce-Ce.

With a sarcastic look on her face, Nevaeh said, "Duhhh, because you're leaving us, and we're going to miss you like crazy! ... Just make sure you come back and see us soon."

"Alright Ce-Ce... It's time to get going. I don't want to get caught outside while it's dark," said Ms. Velma.

As they drove away from the cottage, Ce-Ce looked back one last time as the girls waved, and she blew kisses to them as tears rolled down her face.

The Search Begins

Pacing back and forth in the family room, Ray's mind raced as he tried to figure out a way to find his grand-daughter.

"Sweetie just relax," said Honey as she walked pass the family room. "We can call the state to find out where she's been all these years. There should be some record of who received custody of her."

"But what if she's....," Ray stopped mid-sentence.

Honey turned around and walked in the family room with a look of concern on her face. "What if she's what Ray...?" asked Honey.

"What if she's dead, or living out of the state, or even out of the country?!!" Ray exclaimed.

Walking up to Ray and putting her hand on his shoulder, Honey said, "Baby, you can't expect the worse, we have to remain optimistic and believe we'll find her. Just stay positive... Please."

Taking a deep sigh, Ray looked up at Honey and said, "You're right... I'm just still puzzled to why Bianca wouldn't tell us about Cecilia. Just want to get the opportunity to embrace my granddaughter."

Finally Home

"Whew! I didn't know you had that much stuff child," said Ms. Velma as she sat the last of Ce-Ce's things down in her room.

Laughing at Ms. Velma, Ce-Ce said, "That's the same thing the girls said while we were packing up. I didn't realize it either, but I guess most of it can be thrown out."

Looking at all of Ce-Ce's things, Ms. Velma said, "Well, I'll leave that up to you... but I won't say that I disagree."

"I guess I'll get started putting my things up... It's been a long day!" Said Ce-Ce.

Shaking her head in agreement, Ms. Velma said, "It certainly has Ce-Ce, but tomorrow may be even longer. I have to take you to be enrolled in school, so get your room together, shower, and dinner will be ready soon."
Sitting on the edge of her bed, Ce-Ce nodded her head and said, "Ok Na-Na... I'm on it."

"Ahhhhhh...!!" Waking up out of her sleep, Ce-Ce let out a loud yawn as she stretched and wiped the sleep from her eyes.
As she sat up in the bed, she could smell the sweetness of bacon being cooked, as Na-Na prepared breakfast like she did every morning.
"Good morning young lady...," said Na-Na as Ce-Ce walked into the kitchen to sit down. "Ummm, did you shower and clean yourself up...? Asked Na-Na.

Shaking her head and still visibly tired, Ce-Ce said, "No Ma'am," and turned around to go shower.

"Ok Ce-Ce, I need you to speed it up in there... We have a lot of running around to do today," said Na-Na. She continued, "So come eat breakfast while I get myself together, and we can head up to Union High to get you enrolled.

Walking into the kitchen, Ce-Ce had a concerned look on her face, she said, "Na-Na... Did you say Union High? I've heard some NOT too good things about that school."

While wiping down the counters, Na-Na said, "You will be just fine! Every child in this neighborhood go to that school. You'll make a ton of friends in no time."

Na-Na was a little out of touch with reality and didn't understand the environment of Union High. Ce-Ce had very good reasons about not wanting to go there.

"Can we look at some other schools in the area?" Ce-Ce softly asked.

Hearing the concern in Ce-Ce's voice, Na-Na said, "We'll go to the school to see how everything is. If it's not up to par, then we'll look elsewhere. Deal Cecilia Adams?

With a huge smile on her face, an excited Ce-Ce said, "DEAL!"

Chapter 8

<u>The Unexpected</u>

As Ray came back in the house from taking the cooler to the car, he yelled up the stairs, "Babe, come on we have to drop these things off at the park, so we can get everything set up for the barbeque."

The community barbecue was an annual event that took place during the Labor Day weekend, it promoted non-violence, love, and a time to remember those who died from gun violence within the community.

"I'm coming down Sweetie... Just trying to get my hair together," said Honey as she tried to move quickly.

Laughing at Honey as he carried the last few bags outside to the car, Ray said, "As hot as it is out here, it doesn't matter what you do to your hair babe."

"Whatever Ray Watkins!!" Yelled Honey.

As Na-Na walked outside on the porch, she could feel the excitement in the air as the neighborhood prepared itself for the "***Healing in the Hood***" annual Labor Day barbecue at Peterson Park.

Just a block away from the park, she could smell the aroma of barbecue in the air while Earth, Wind, and Fire's song September played loudly.

"Good morning Ms. Velma!" Yelled Mr. Archibald from across the street as he watered his flowers.

Thomas Archibald was a retired postal worker that has lived in the neighborhood for over 30 years. His wife Vera Maye passed away 5 years ago, and his two daughters Chantel and Erikka moved out of state after they graduated from college.

"Good morning Mr. Archibald. How are you doing today?" Replied Ms. Velma.

Covering his eyes from the sun, Mr. Archibald said, "I'm doing well this fine morning. This is a perfect day for the neighborhood barbecue, we couldn't have picked a better one."

Standing with her hands on her hips as she listened to Mr. Archibald, Ms. Velma said, "I agree with you Thomas, I just hope it doesn't get too hot out here today like it did last year."

While Mr. Archibald and Ms. Velma were talking, Ce-Ce came out onto the porch and sat on the steps.

As Ce-Ce sat there, she dazed off into a deep thought. Watching the birds and the squirrels battle it out in the tree's, all while thinking about how she has a home with Ms. Velma.

Looking down at Ce-Ce, Ms. Velma said, "Good morning sweetie... Are you ok?" Looks like you were in a deep thought.

With a slight shrug, Ce-Ce replied, "I'm good Na-Na, just chilling... That's all."

"Good. Now chill yourself on in the shower, so we can get ready to go down to the neighborhood barbecue," said Ms. Velma.

Putting her head down, so the sun can hit the back of her neck, Ce-Ce said, "Ok Na-Na... I'm about to head in, but I don't know why I need to shower, because I'm gonna get super sweaty from playing ball."

While shaking her head as she turned to go in the house, Ms. Velma said, "Well at least you won't be musty, now come on and get in the shower young lady."

As the cars filled the parking lot, and spilled over onto the grass at Peterson Park, the day was destined to be a success. DJ Xtract had the music blasting and the grill masters cooked the food while bobbing their heads to the GAP BAND that played loudly through the airwaves.

"Look at all these people Na-Na," said Ce-Ce as they walked up to the park.

With a slight giggle, Ms. Velma said, "Child, this ain't half of the folks that will be here within the next couple of hours. You better gon' head and get to the basketball courts, because it's already getting full."

As Ce-Ce took off running towards the basketball courts, she yelled, "See you later Na-Na! I'll be over to eat once I'm done giving these clowns buckets..."

"Oh, wow babe, it's filling up quick out here... Let's hurry up and find a decent parking spot," said Honey as Ray pulled up to Peterson Park.

While pulling up on the grass and focusing on backing the car in, Ray said, "No worries Honey, I'm going to pull in right next to this tent where Chuck is. We'll be grilling with him and his family today. He saved a spot for us."

"Ray! What's up bro? Glad you all came out!" Said an excited Chuck as Ray and Honey got out of the car.

With a huge smile on his face, Ray gave Chuck a handshake and hug while saying, "It's good to see you too bro. It's been a long time, and it's good to be back in the neighborhood."

Ray and Chuck took the bags out of the car, so they could get started on grilling the food.

"Hey Chuck, please tell me that you brought the television out here... Michigan is playing Western Michigan at 12... I don't want to miss it," said Ray.

Looking at Ray as if to say, 'Are you stupid,' Chuck said, "Come on bro, you know good and well I brought the television, especially on the first weekend of college football!'

Laughing at Chuck, Ray said, "You are right bro, I should have known better..."
"Now come on and let's get this grill going!' Said Chuck.

The sun was starting to come out more, and the temperature began to rise while more people flooded Peterson Park. Many came to the basketball court to either watch or with hopes of getting a chance to play.

"Yo! Are we gonna play ball or shoot-around all day? Y'all could've stayed at home in your backyards for that!" Yelled Tom-Tom to the people on the court.

Walking up to Tom-Tom, Ce-Ce said, "Big T, I'm on first, so count me in."

Shaking his head and chuckling at the same time, Tom-Tom said, "So I see you finally decided to come back huh? I got you though, you can run on my team."

"Well thank you Sir... Just make sure you get me the ball. No time for losing today... You hear me? (In her Chris Tucker voice) Do-you-understand-the-words-that-are-coming-out-of-my-mouth?!" Said Ce-Ce jokingly.

While walking away from Ce-Ce and laughing, Tom-Tom said, "Something is really wrong with you lil girl... Just make sure you're ready to play!"

Like times before, the buzz shot through the park about this little girl destroying any and every one that stepped on the court. People left their tents and grills to see what all the fuss was about.

Sitting down watching the football game under the tent, Ray noticed everyone walking towards the basketball courts. He looked at Honey and Chuck and said, "What's all the commotion, and where is everyone going?"

With his eyes fixed on the television and sitting up in his chair in anticipation, Chuck said, "Everybody is talking about this little girl at the courts giving everybody buckets, so they're going over there to watch."
"A little girl?" Said Ray...

Clearing her throat, Honey said, "Ummm what does that supposed to mean? Little girls can't play basketball?"

"No-No-No, not like that babe... You know what I meant..." Said Ray trying to clear up the comment he made.

"I mean, we can go take a look... Michigan has this win in the bag, so let's go see what all the talk is about," said Chuck.

"Come on, let's go Chuck... Ladies, we'll be right back," said Ray to Honey and Chuck's wife, and they walked over to the basketball courts.

"Bro, will somebody check her?? Stop acting like y'all scared of her!!" Yelled Zay at his teammates in the huddle.

Isaiah Crenshaw, who everybody in the hood called Zay, had a wiry frame, and was very athletic. He played ball at Union High back in the day but got into some trouble that unfortunately ended his basketball career.
Clapping his hands loudly as he stood next to their huddle, Tom-Tom hollered out, "It don't matter how much you yell, it's not gonna change the outcome of this game my guy!"

"Tom-Tom, you're being real disrespectful right now... Respect the game homeboy! Respect the game!" yelled Zay as they came out of the huddle.

"I got her!" Hollered Zay... As he pointed at Ce-Ce.

Despite the hard defense Zay played on Ce-Ce, she still managed to get the ball. Her composure never changed, neither did she get rattled by all the antics Zay did.

Ray and Chuck walked up to the court, and somehow pressed their way through the crowd to get close to the end of the court.

"Pop-pop-pop-pop," said Ce-Ce as she hit Zay with a dribble combo, step back, SWISH!

Ray stood in amazement as if he couldn't believe what he was seeing. In a weird way, it was like he was watching RJ play...

Ray looked at Chuck and said, "Are you seeing what I'm seeing? Who is this little girl, and where did she come from?"

"I guess that is the million dollar question bro... It's not the first time she's been around here though," said Chuck.

Still taken back, Ray says, "Bro, I haven't seen nothing like this in 15 years... What is her name? Who is she here with?"

Turning and asking the guy standing next to him, Chuck said, "They say her name is Ce-Ce, but they don't know who she is here with.

"Ce-Ce?? As in Cecilia??" Ray thought to himself out loud.

Then he thought to himself, "There is no way this is who I think it is..."

Ray pulled out his phone and called Honey..., "Babe, get over here to the basketball courts right now!"

"Sweety what is wrong?" Replied Honey.

"I will explain it to you as soon as you get over here... Just hurry up," said Ray.

Honey finally made it through the crowd to Ray, and she noticed the intense look on his face.

"Ummm babe, are you ok?? Because I haven't seen that look on your face since...," said Honey.

Looking at the basketball court, and spotting this caramel skinned, wavy haired girl out there angelically gliding across the court.
"OH MY GOD..." Thought Honey as she watched Ce-Ce play ball... "This can't be, she looks just like my baby...," she thought again, but this time out loud.

Ray looked over at Honey, and he noticed her eyes watering up.

"Are you thinking what I'm thinking sweetheart?" Asked Ray.

"I think I am babe...," Honey said as she stood there motionless.

With a curious look on his face, Chuck asked, "Ok, what's going on with you two? Because you're acting kinda strange..."

Hearing the question asked by Chuck, but ignoring him at the same time, Honey asked, "Babe, do you know her name...?

With his hand on his forehead while feeling perplexed, Ray replied, "Ce-Ce... They said her name is Ce-Ce..."

Silence....

Chapter 9

As the game ended, Ray tried to get to Ce-Ce, but she was gone and nowhere to be found.

Ray walked up to Tom-Tom and said, "Hey, what's up man... The little girl that was on your team, where did she go?"

Tom-Tom recognized Ray's face... "Hey, you're RJ Watkins' father! I played against him in High School, and NOBODY could do anything with that cat on the court!"

With a humbled look on his face, and the pain of losing RJ still stinging, Ray said, "Yes, I'm his father, and thank you for the kind words. RJ had a special gift, and he was my world."

Ray paused as if he went into a deep thought, then he looked back up at Tom-Tom and said, "The little girl... Do you know where she went?" Laughing... Tom-Tom said, "Mr. Watkins, that girl is like an angel... She appears and disappears like nothing I've ever seen before. I heard she's supposed to be living with Ms. Velma now... She lives down the street on Coyle, just a block over.

"I greatly appreciate that... Oh, by the way, great game out there," said Ray. "Yes Sir, thank you Mr. Watkins and great meeting you," replied Tom-Tom.

High School

As summer was coming to an end, Ms. Velma still didn't know what High School she was going to send Ce-Ce to.

Because Ce-Ce was a talented basketball player, Ms. Velma thought about sending her to Kingdom Prep where athletics was just as important as academics. However, Ms. Velma couldn't afford the tuition for Ce-Ce to attend.

While sitting at the dinner table trying to figure what was best for Ce-Ce and how she was going to make it happen, Ms. Velma's phone rang.

"Hello..." Answered Ms. Velma.

The voice on the other line said, "Velma! How are you doing? This is Vanessa Whittier."

With shock and excitement in her voice, Ms. Velma said, "Oh my GOD! Vanessa is that you?? How have you been? I'm just sitting here trying to figure what school to send Ce-Ce to... I've been racking my brain ALL morning!"

"Ce-Ce?" asked Vanessa.

"Oh yes, I'm sorry girl, I adopted a young lady about a month ago. Her name is Cecilia, we call her Ce-Ce for short," said Ms. Velma.

"Oh, that is beautiful Velma! You always spoke about adopting one day, and here you are doing just what you said you were going to do," replied Vanessa.

Sitting at the table with her hand on her head, Ms. Velma said, "She's a special girl Vanessa, I just want to make sure she gets the proper education, so I don't want to drop the ball with her."

"Velma, have you forgotten that Rudolph is the Headmaster at Kingdom Prep High School? You're one of my best friends, so you know he can get her in school there if that's something you're interested in," said Vanessa.

Rudolph C. Whittier has been the Headmaster at Kingdom Prep High School for the 25 years of the school's existence, and he's Vanessa's husband of almost 35 years.

Shaking her head, Ms. Velma responded, "Vanessa, I totally forgot about that. I literally mentioned Kingdom Prep about an hour ago, and I thought to myself, there is NO WAY I can afford to send Ce-Ce there. She is a PHENOMENAL basketball player Vanessa... You would have to see it to believe it."

"Well, you know they pride themselves on Academic-Athletics at that school... They've had one of the top programs in the country for years, and it's only getting better," said Vanessa.

Knowing that God had just answered her prayer, Ms. Velma said without hesitation, "Just tell me what I need to do and where I need to be, if Rudolph can do anything to help us Vanessa... I TRULY appreciate you; I really do!"

The Conversation

As Chuck worked in his garage, he got a call from Ray saying that he was in the neighborhood and he wanted to stop by.

When Ray pulled up to Chuck's house he sat in the car for a little while, while his mind raced about Ce-Ce and the possibility of her being his granddaughter.

While Chuck was pulling his trash containers to the curb, he noticed that Ray was still sitting in his car.

Knocking on the car window, Chuck asked, "Hey bro, are you alright in there?"

While nodding his head as to say yes, Ray opened the door and got out of the car.

"What's going on bro? You good...?" asked Chuck.

"Just a lot on my mind Chuck... that's all," said Ray.

Leaning up against the car, Chuck looked at Ray and said, "Well, do you care to talk about it? Especially if you drove all the way out here from Novi... You're not just 'In the neighborhood' bro. So, tell me what's up."
Taking a deep sigh... Ray said, "The little girl..."

Puzzled by what he was referring to, Chuck said, "What little girl?"

"At the park bro, the little girl that was playing basketball at the neighborhood barbeque," said Ray.

With a confused look on his face, Chuck said, "Oook... What about her? You and Honey was acting weird that day. What was up with that?"

"Bro, I don't know how to say this... I think that little girl is my granddaughter. I believe she's RJ's daughter...," said Ray.

"What?!! You think what?!!" Exclaimed Chuck.

Shaking his head, Ray said, "Yea Chuck, you heard me right... I believe that little girl Ce-Ce is my son's daughter."

Rubbing his forehead as if he was trying to gather his thoughts, Chuck said, "How? How is that even possible bro? Why would you even think something like that is even possible?"

Ray went on to tell Chuck how Bianca stopped by the house and told him and Honey about the pregnancy, and how she never told anyone she was pregnant, and that she left the baby at the hospital.

Chuck couldn't believe what he was hearing, thinking back on watching Ce-Ce play ball, he knew that there was something special about her.
"So, what are you going to do? What's next bro?" Asked Chuck.

Rubbing his head with both hands, Ray said, "I was contemplating going to their home and knocking on the door, but I want to talk to Bianca again before I contact them."

Shaking his head in agreement, Chuck said, "That sounds like a good idea bro... Maybe you should consider taking Bianca with you."

"Yea... We'll see bro... We'll see." Said Ray.

Chapter 10

Kingdom Prep

"Well don't you look nice this morning Ms. Cecilia Adams..." Said Ms. Velma with a huge smile on her face as Ce-Ce walked in the family room.

Shaking her head with a bashful but blushing face, Ce-Ce replied, "Thank you Na-Na."

It was finally Ce-Ce's first day of school, and she was fortunate to receive financial assistance from the ***Powertrain Endowment Fund*** to attend Kingdom Prep, thanks to Mr. Whittier's relationship with the CEO of the company.

While grabbing her keys off the table, Ms. Velma looked at Ce-Ce and said, "Ok sweetie, are you ready to get to school? We're going to meet with Mr. Whittier, get your schedule, and then you'll be all set to go to class." Shrugging her shoulders, Ce-Ce said, "Yea Na-Na, I'm as ready as I'll ever be..."

The Arrival

"Look at this place...." Said Ms. Velma as she pulled up to Kingdom Prep. Kingdom Prep was second to none, and for some reason it felt like déjà vu to Ce-Ce, as if she's been to KPA before.
They both were in awe of the beautiful landscaping and how clean the school was, as if you could eat off the ground.

They sat in the car looking at each other in amazement... Ms. Velma broke the ice by saying, "Come on sweetie, let's get you enrolled in school and meet Mr. Whittier..."

Taking a deep sigh, Ce-Ce said, "Ok Na-Na... I'm ready."

As Ce-Ce and Ms. Velma walked into the building, they could feel the anxiety in the air with the new school year starting.

Students were quickly moving through the hallways, and the sound of lockers closing and chatter of friends seeing each other for the first time since the end of the last school year filled the air.

"Oh my God! Excuse me!" Said Ce-Ce as she mistakenly bumped into a young lady.

As the young lady kneeled to pick up her books that fell to the floor, Ce-Ce hurried to help her pick them up.

"Let me help you..." said Ce-Ce while looking down at the books.
As Ce-Ce looked over she said with excitement, "Zae!!! Is that really you??"

Looking over and realizing who Ce-Ce was, Zae shouted, "Ce-Ce!!!!! What are you doing here? Oh my God, it's SO GOOD to see you!"
While laughing and hugging each other, Ce-Ce replied, "My Na-Na didn't want me at Union High or any of the other public schools, so somehow I ended up here. Besides, I heard they're hoop team is pretty good.

Smiling as she listened to Ce-Ce talk, Zae said, "You've always been good at basketball... I think you were born to do it, which has always been dope."

Looking back at Ce-Ce, Ms. Velma said, "Come on Ce-Ce, we have to meet with Mr. Whittier now... We're running late.

"It was good seeing you Zae, and I'm glad I have at least one friend here!" Said Ce-Ce.

"Same here Ce-Ce... This school is a haven for the bougie people, so I'm glad you're here as well. Let's get together at lunch, and you never know, we may have some classes together!" Said Zae.

"Let's keep our fingers crossed," replied Ce-Ce as she walked away.

"So, I see you're already making friends...." Said Ms. Velma.

Still smiling from seeing Zae, Ce-Ce said with excitement, "No Na-Na, that's Zae from CCG! She goes to school here! Well, I guess I shouldn't be surprised because her parents have a lot of money, so it makes sense."

"Well, it's good you have someone here that you know... That should make things a little easier for you," said Ms. Velma.

As they walked into the office a deep voice rang out, "Ms. Velma!!"

It was Rudolph Whittier the Headmaster at Kingdom Prep.

"Mr. Rudolph Whittier!" Said Ms. Velma as she hugged him.

Looking over at Ce-Ce, Mr. Whittier said, "So this is Ms. Cecilia Adams... How are you doing today young lady? Welcome to Kingdom Prep Academy... We are excited to have you here."

With a bashful look on her face, Ce-Ce said, "Thank you Sir... I'm excited to be here as well."

"I also heard that you're quite the basketball player... I haven't seen people light up about a basketball player when they talk about them, since this one kid we had here named R.J. Watkins. He was a rare and special talent... His life was cut short... Ahhh, I can't even talk about it. Such a tragedy..." Said Mr. Whittier.

Nodding her head, Ms. Velma said, "I remember that... It was sad and senseless the way they murdered that boy... The annual neighborhood barbeque at Peterson Park every summer is to honor him and others."

"Yes Ma'am... I never knew that." Said Ce-Ce.

"Well, you'll see a lot of R.J. Watkins around the school and the gymnasium. He was a beloved son of Kingdom Prep as well as the city of Detroit, so we honored him by naming the basketball court after him." Said Mr. Whittier.

For some strange reason as Ce-Ce listened to the story and legend of R.J. Watkins, an eerie feeling came over her, as if a ghost walked the hallways of the school.

Good First Day

As the day went on Ce-Ce fell in love with Kingdom Prep more and more.

The atmosphere, culture, and climate of the school was perfect. Especially for any student that was just starting high school.

While Ce-Ce sat in her desk waiting for the dismissal bell to ring, Zae leaned over to her and asked, "Hey Ce-Ce, what are you doing after school?"

Looking over at Zae, Ce-Ce said, "I'm going by the gym to meet the Athletic Director, so I can find out when the girl's team will be practicing."

Letting out a loud exhale, Zae said, "I do not want to go home... Maybe I should come with you..."

"Why not? What's wrong...? Asked Ce-Ce.

Shaking her head, Zae replied, "A lot Ce-Ce... Some days I wish I could just disappear or even go back to CCG."
"You mean to tell me it's that bad? That you would rather go back to Hawthorne?" Asked Ce-Ce.

"Yep..." Replied Zae dryly.

"Look Zae, just come with me to the gym, hopefully they're playing after school and you can watch. Nothing like moral support!" Said Ce-Ce as she let out a laugh.

Laughing at Ce-Ce's comment, Zae said, "No problem, I got you Ce-Ce...

Maybe I can be the President of the Cecilia Adam's fan club!"
"Sound's good to me!" Said a laughing Ce-Ce.

As the bell sounded and everyone grabbed their things to leave school for the day, Mrs. Nottingham called Ce-Ce up to her desk.

Mrs. Nottingham was a short heavy set lady that sported a short haircut, and she wore wired glasses. She's been teaching at Kingdom Prep for 20 years, and she's a school favorite amongst the student body.

As Ce-Ce walked up to the desk, Zae followed not too far behind.

Mrs. Nottingham asked, "Cecilia, are you related to Bianca Elise by any chance? You look just like her... She's one of my former students, and you're a splitting image of her."

With a confused look on her face, Ce-Ce replied, "No Ma'am, I don't know who a Biii..."

Interrupting her to help her pronounce the name, Mrs. Nottingham said, "Bianca... Bianca Elise."

"Right... I don't know who that is... Sorry Mrs. Nottingham." Said Ce-Ce.

"No need to apologize dear... I was willing to bet that you were her daughter. She was beautiful just like you are, and I tell ya', she was crazy about that R.J. Watkins kid," said Mrs. Nottingham.

Looking at Mrs. Nottingham with big eyes, Ce-Ce asked, "Are you talking about the basketball player that was murdered? That R.J. Watkins?

"Oh, you know about him?" Asked Mrs. Nottingham.

"Yea...., and It's kinda creeping me out, because I just heard about him today from Mr. Whittier. He was pretty popular I heard," said Ce-Ce.

Shaking her head in agreement, "Popular is an understatement when speaking about R.J. Watkins, he's more of a legend around here. The buzz that went on around here about him was like no other, and he was such a HUMBLE kid. Very kind young man."

"Sounds like he was special to everyone... Well, I have to go meet with the Athletic Director Mrs. Nottingham. Can you tell me how to get to the gym?" Asked Ce-Ce.
Mrs. Nottingham gave her the directions to the Athletic Director's office that was across from the gymnasium, and she told Ce-Ce, "If you want to learn more about R.J. Watkins, you can ask Coach Boyd... He coached R.J. when he played here."

"Will do Mrs. Nottingham, Thank you!" Said Ce-Ce.

As they walked out of the classroom, Zae asked Ce-Ce, "What was that all about...?

With a blank look on her face, Ce-Ce said, "I have no idea...."

Chapter 11

As Honey prepared dinner in the kitchen, and Ray sat in the family room watching the L.A. Dodgers and San Francisco Giants play in the MLB playoffs, there was a knock at the door.

Ray jumped up off the couch to answer the door, as he opened it, it was Bianca.

"Hey Bianca! Glad you could come by, there's something me and Honey want to speak to you about..., said Ray.

With an uncertain look on her face, but at the same time feeling nervous, Bianca said, "Hey Mr. Watkins, and ooook...."

"No need to be nervous," said Ray while laughing, "Come on in," he continued.

"Hey sweetie," said Honey as she came out of the kitchen and gave Bianca a hug.

"Hey Mrs. Watkins, how are you?" Replied Bianca.

Looking at Bianca, Honey said, "I'm doing ok, no complaints. Just finishing up dinner, and you're more than welcome to have some if you want."

Shaking her head to politely refuse, Bianca said, "No thank you Mrs. Watkins, I ate before I came over."

As they all sat down, Ray said, "I know you're wondering why we called you over here Bianca, but we feel like we've stumbled upon something, and we wanted to share it with you.

Looking confused and wondering where Ray was going with what he was trying to say, Bianca said, "Oook... I'm listening Mr. Watkins..."

Ray took a deep breath as he tried to put his words together... "Um... Last week while we were at the neighborhood barbeque at Peterson Park, there was this basketball player out on the court that had the whole park buzzing."

Still confused about what he was trying to say, Bianca said, "Mr. Watkins, no disrespect, but what does this have to do with me?"

Sighing, Ray said, "It was a little girl. The basketball player was a little girl...."

Not able to keep her composure any longer, Honey yelled out, "We believe we found Cecilia! Bianca, we believe we found you and R.J.'s daughter, and our granddaughter!"

With tears filling up in her eyes, Bianca said, "Mr. and Mrs. Watkins... What are you all saying? You're telling me that you believe you found my little girl?? Are you sure?"
"Bianca, like my wife said, we believe it is her. She's a splitting image of you, and she can REALLY play basketball... They also called her Ce-Ce, which I believe is short for Cecilia... What are the odds of that?" Exclaimed Ray.

Bianca sat back on the sofa and looked up at the ceiling while putting her hands on her head, as she tried to wrap her mind around what Ray just told her.

Looking over at Ray, Bianca asked, "Where is she Mr. Watkins? Did you all get a chance to talk to her? Who was she with?"

"As soon as the game was over, she disappeared... I tried to find her, and I asked around about her whereabouts, but nobody knew...," said Ray.

They sat in silence as everyone's thoughts were the same... Where is Cecilia? Is it Cecilia? What if it's not Cecilia...?

Meeting Coach Boyd

When Ce-Ce went to meet with Coach Boyd after school earlier in the week, he was not in his office because he had a family emergency.

Coach Boyd's mother had grown ill, and the doctor told him there was nothing else they could do for her and sent her home on hospice care.

Mildred Boyd was 92 years old, and she was the oldest of 13 children. Her parents moved to Detroit in the late 1920's to work in the automotive industry from South Carolina. Marcellus Boyd, whom she was married to for 47 years died five years ago from a massive heart attack in his sleep, he was 87 years old.

Being the only child, Coach Boyd knew the stress of burying a parent and taking on the responsibility of making sure everything was in place.

As Coach Boyd sat in his office, there was a knock at his door. When he looked up, he sees this caramel skinned young lady with wavy hair.

"Hello young lady, may I help you?" Asked Coach Boyd.

"Hi.... Are you Coach Boyd?" Sheepishly asked Ce-Ce.

Sarcastically looking at the name plate on his desk, Coach Boyd said, "I believe so..."

Shaking her head in embarrassment, Ce-Ce said, "Ok, dumb question...

Anyway, my name is Cecilia Adams and I'm interested in playing basketball. I was told to come see you the first day of school, but when I came you weren't here."

"Yes... Mr. Whittier told me about you, and he spoke very highly of you... Where have you played?" Asked Coach Boyd.

"I haven't played on an actual team, I only play on the playground or at the local recreation center by my old placement," said Ce-Ce.
"Did you say placement? What do you mean by placement?" Asked Coach Boyd.

"Yes, my placement. I lived at the Covenant Center for Girls, until I was adopted earlier this year." Said Ce-Ce.

Sitting up in his chair to look out of his office door, Coach Boyd asked, "Who is that standing out there...?"

Peeking her head around the corner to look in, Zae said, "Hi Coach Boyd, my name is Zae, I don't play basketball, I'm just here in support of Ce-Ce."

Looking at Ce-Ce, Coach Boyd said, "So your friends call you Ce-Ce...? Ok, Ce-Ce... The girls will be playing at 4:15 today, and I'll let Coach Law know that you'll be participating today."

With a huge smile on her face, Ce-Ce said, 'Thank you Coach Boyd!!"

"Ahhh, don't thank me just yet... Our girls' team is pretty good. They've been to the State Championship game the last two years, and they have a great shot of going again this year." Said Coach Boyd.

Hearing what Coach Boyd said, Ce-Ce said, "You said went... You said the girls team went to the State Championship game... Correct?"

Nodding his head in agreement, Coach Boyd said, "Correct they went to the State Championship game the past two years."

"That's what I thought you said... No worries, I'm here now, so we'll win it this year instead of just 'going'," said Ce-Ce.

Coach Boyd marveled at Ce-Ce... He hadn't seen this kind of confidence in a kid in a long time.

As Coach Boyd goes in his closet, he asked Ce-Ce what jersey number she wanted to wear.

Ce-Ce quickly replied, "I want to wear number 24!!"

Taken back by what she said, Coach Boyd said, "I'm sorry Ce-Ce... Nobody can ever wear that jersey number again here at Kingdom Prep. We're actually having a ceremony this year to retire it forever."

Ce-Ce thought to herself... "Is it because of Kobe Bryant?" Then it hit her... "Let me guess... R.J. Watkins?" Ce-Ce said to Coach Watkins.

Shocked that she mentioned that name, Coach Boyd said, "You know about R.J.?"

Shaking her head, Ce-Ce sarcastically said, "Do I know about him...? That's all I've been hearing about since I got to this school... You all 'literally' worship the ground he walked on..."

Coach Boyd walked back over to his chair... Sat down. Folded his arms and looked off as if he was in deep thought. He went on to say...
"I remember getting the call... R.J. had come back to the city to surprise his mother... It was her birthday. I had just gotten back home from taking my father to the doctor, for his yearly check-up. I'll never forget the trimmer in his father's voice as he told me R.J. was gone... "They killed my boy!! They

killed my boy!!" He said that repeatedly... It played in my head for years.... Cecilia... We don't worship the ground R.J. walked on; we HONOR the ground he walked on... Some people are too good for this world, and R.J. Watkins was one of those people. Please excuse me for a minute..."

Not really grasping the magnitude of how R.J.'s life and death impacted Kingdom Prep, yet Ce-Ce understood that he was a special individual, and the success and fame he accomplished there set the culture in athletics, especially basketball, at Kingdom Prep.

Basketball Workouts

While walking into the gymnasium, Ce-Ce stared at the banners that hung in the rafters, and she counted a total of 18 State Championships between the girls' and boys' basketball teams.

Looking over at Coach Boyd, Ce-Ce said... "Hey Coach, you didn't tell me that y'all won all these championships!"

"I know Ce-Ce... We don't hang our hat on the past, but on what we're doing now...," said Coach Boyd.

"Ladies let's go! You all should be dressed and on the court! School let out 20 minutes ago!" Said Coach Law.

Coach Dennis Law garnered instant success at Kingdom Prep, he inherited a very talented team, but was able to recruit at a high level because of his charisma, and ability to relate to young people. Coach Law stood at 6 foot 10 inches tall, and he was a High School and College All-American that played 15 years professionally before retiring 2 years ago. His passion for the game was unmatched, and his teams embodied that mentality.

As Coach Boyd and Ce-Ce stood against the wall, Coach Law walked over to them and said, "Boyd! What's good bro? I see you have someone for me..." Looking down at Ce-Ce, Coach Law continued... "You sure this is something you want to do? This ain't for everybody sweetie.?

With a slight smile on her face, but a look as if she was just insulted..., Ce-Ce replied, "Well Coach, the good thing is, I'm not everybody... I'm sure this is what I want to do."

With a shocked look on his face, and extending his hand out to give Ce-Ce a fist pound, Coach Law said, "Wooooord? It's like that young lady? Ok, I like her Boyd... What's your name?"

Looking Coach Law in the eye, Ce-Ce said, "My name is Cecilia Adams, and it's nice to meet you Coach...."

"Coach Law, you can call me Coach Law..." He replied.

"Well, do you have gym clothes and a jersey?" Asked Coach Law.

Interrupting the conversation, Coach Boyd said, "Yea Law, I got her squared away, so she's good to go."

Coach Law blew his whistle, and he called the girls into a huddle to introduce Ce-Ce to the team.

"Everyone, this is Cecilia Adams and she will be working out with us today in hopes of playing on the team...," said Coach Law.

All the girls were very receptive and welcomed Ce-Ce with open arms, but on the court, it was going to be a battle.

The culture and climate that Coach Law built at Kingdom Prep was a competitive one, where he stressed that "Nothing is given, everything is earned, and you work for what you want."

"Ok ladies let's get it going! All I ask is that everyone compete at a high level, and that you make each other better..." Said Coach Law.

As the workouts went on Coach Law could tell that Ce-Ce was something special. She played at another level, especially for an incoming freshman.

The college coaches that watched the team play was highly impressed with Ce-Ce, they couldn't believe she was only 14 years old.
Ce-Ce came down the court and did a cross-over between the legs move that made arguably the best player on Kingdom Prep's team Nychella Campbell fall...

Everyone in the gym went crazy, and Zae jumped up and screamed, "Let's GO Ce-Ce!!"

Coach Law called the ladies into a huddle when they finished playing, and he's never been at a loss for words before, but today was different.

"Um... Um... Wow... Where did you play at last year? Middle school? AAU?" Asked Coach Law.

Whipping the sweat off her face, Ce-Ce said, "Nowhere Coach... I just played at the rec center or on the playgrounds in the city."

Still dumbfounded and speechless, Coach Law said, "Well, I haven't seen anything like this in a very long time... I believe all the college coaches that were here today feel the same way. Where are you from again...?

Letting out a slight chuckle, Ce-Ce said, "I told you Coach, I'm from Detroit. I lived in a girl's home for most or all of my life, and I fell in love with basketball when I was watching it one day... Once I seen it, I felt like I could do it... Now I live with Ms. Velma... She adopted me."

Coach Law looked over at Coach Boyd as he watched from the sidelines, and Coach Boyd laughed and shrugged his shoulders and said, "Hey I told you they said she was special..."

"OH MY GOD Ce-Ce!! That was dope!!" Said an excited Zae as she ran over from the bleachers.

Looking at Zae in amazement, Coach Law said, "You have your own fan club I see..."

Shaking her head while laughing, Ce-Ce said, "Stop it Coach! This is my friend Zae, she just supports me, that's all."

"Yea, I hear ya'! You keep playing like you did today, you're going to have the whole city behind you!" Said Coach Law.

As the girls were walking to the locker room Ce-Ce looked over at Nychella and jokingly said, "Hey superstar, you may wanna wear those ankle braces tomorrow..."

Nychella put her head down and laughed... "Yea, you got me today, but your day is coming newbie!"

All the girls laughed as they went into the locker room to get changed.

Chapter 12

It was a cool cloudy day, but the excitement was high at Kingdom Prep, because for the first time in 10 years they would be playing Union High School this week, which was the top Public School League team for the past 5 years. Coach Udonis Mitchell had built a strong program at his alma mater, and took it personal when Ce-Ce decided to attend Kingdom Prep.

Udonis Mitchell was a neighborhood hero and considered one of the best athletes to come out of Detroit. His only connection to Kingdom Prep was R.J. Watkins, because they played AAU basketball together on the Nike circuit in high school. Mitch played basketball at Michigan State University and finished his career as the all-time leader in points and assist. He often tells people if R.J. Watkins wouldn't have died, he would've had a better career than him, because he was a special talent. He started coaching girls' basketball when the legendary Henry Macon suddenly died 6 years ago while collapsing during a game.

As Ce-Ce walked in the school, she spotted Zae. They haven't been able to spend as much time together as they used to because of the basketball season.

"Zae! Zae!" Yelled Ce-Ce.

Zae kept walking fast up the hallway.

Ce-Ce ran to catch up to Zae, and she reached out and grabbed her arm.

"OUCH!! Don't do that!" Shouted Zae.

With a shocked look on her face, Ce-Ce asked, "What's going on with you Zae? You didn't hear me calling you...? What's wrong with your arm, and why do you have those glasses on??"

"Look I'm fine Ce-Ce.... No need to worry about me..." Said Zae.

In one motion Ce-Ce snatched the glasses off Zae's face, and what she seen froze her in place.

"Zae... What happened to your face...? Who did this to you?!" Asked Ce-Ce with tears swelling up in her eyes.

Zae broke down and started crying in the middle of the hallway, and Mr. Whittier noticed it while standing in the office.

Coming to the door, Mr. Whittier said, "Hey you two, is everything ok?"

Visibly emotional as well, Ce-Ce turned to Mr. Whittier and said, "Yes Sir, we're ok, just girl stuff..."

With a look of concern on his face, Mr. Whittier said, "Very well, get to class before you're late."

Part of Ce-Ce wanted to say something to Mr. Whittier, but the other part wanted to protect her friend.
Turning back around towards Zae, Ce-Ce said, "Come on Zae, let's go to the restroom so I can get you cleaned up."

As they walked in the restroom Ce-Ce made sure that nobody was in any of the stalls, and she locked the bathroom door behind them.

Zae broke down again, but this time it was an uncontrollable cry, and Ce-Ce began to cry with her.

"You have to tell me what's going on Zae... Who did this to you?? Please tell me...," Ce-Ce begged.

Trying to form her words, Zae finally settled down to speak... "It's my dad Ce-Ce... The drug use, the running away, the sex with the boys, it's all a way for me to escape. I HATE him Ce-Ce, he makes me feel like trash, and as if I'm worthless. Why me Ce-Ce?! People see the nice house, cars, and fancy designer clothes, but don't realize what REALLY goes on behind closed doors. I'm afraid to go to sleep at night... The abuse comes in more than one way, it comes in any way he wants it to come. Ce-Ce I lost my virginity at 8 years old!! TO MY FATHER!!!"

Zae cried while Ce-Ce held her and sat crushed from what she just heard.

"Please don't say anything to anyone about this Ce-Ce... PLEASE!" Said Zae.

Nodding her head as if to say ok, Ce-Ce said, "Don't worry Zae, I'm here for you. I promise..."
The tardy bell sounded, and Ce-Ce said, "Come on Zae, hurry up wash your face and put your glasses back on. Everything is going to be ok..."

Exhausted

As Ce-Ce walked in the house, the smell of neckbones, beans, and cornbread filled the air as Ms. Velma cooked in the kitchen, with Ray Charles' *The Right Time* playing loudly throughout the house.

Ce-Ce dropped her bags by the front door and collapsed on the couch face first.

"Is that you Ce-Ce?" Yelling Ms. Velma over the loud music as she walked in the living room to find Ce-Ce laying on the couch.

With a slight chuckle, Ms. Velma said, "I see someone had a long day today!"

Rolling over on her back, Ce-Ce said, "Na-Na... Coach Law be KILLING US! I thought basketball was supposed to be fun..."

Laughing at Ce-Ce, Ms. Velma said, "Well sweetie, this is part of the fun... Especially if you want to win and be the best. You can't want the pleasure without the responsibility."

"I guess Na-Na," said an exhausted Ce-Ce.
As Ms. Velma walked back into the kitchen, she said, "Get off that couch and go get cleaned up baby... Maybe you'll feel better after a hot shower. Hopefully, you finished all of your homework already..."

"Yes, it's all done Na-Na... We had study table after school before Coach Law tortured us in practice...," said Ce-Ce.

"Well good, now go get in the shower so you can eat dinner and get some rest," said Ms. Velma.

Game Day

"Is it always this crazy on game days?" Asked Ce-Ce.

Laughing at Ce-Ce because she looked like a dear in head lights, Nychella said, "Girl, you haven't seen nothing! Wait until all those people get in the gym, you'll think nothing else was going on in the city."

Shrugging her shoulders, Ce-Ce said, "Well, I guess the more people that show up, the bigger the show..."

Nychella looked at Ce-Ce and thought to herself, "This little girl is either REALLY fearless, or she's full of herself..." Either way, she was probably right.

It was game time, and the fieldhouse was jammed packed and there was not one seat in the house. It was standing room only, and every news outlet in the city was in the building.

Everyone wanted to see firsthand what all the talk was about with this freshman named Cecilia Adams. Even though it was over 2000 people in the crowd, Ce-Ce still tried to find Zae, but she didn't see her anywhere in the student session.

"Ce-Ce! Get focused and stop looking in the crowd... You better get used to this young lady." Said Coach Law.

Nodding her head at Coach Law, Ce-Ce said, "I'm all in Coach! Let's get it!!"

The crowd was going crazy as they watched Ce-Ce and Kingdom Prep demolish Union High by 27 points, and they went up as much as 39 points at one time.

Ce-Ce and Nychella was amazing with 24 points and 21 points respectively against a VERY good Union High team.

As they stormed into the locker room screaming at the top of their lungs, Coach Law said, "That's how you make a statement!! That's how you dominate a game from the beginning to the end!!"

He praised Ce-Ce on her play and applauded Nychella on her leadership as a senior, because very rarely will a senior take a backseat to a freshman, but Coach Law instilled in the young ladies that teamwork makes the dream work.

"Ok ladies get dressed and get out of here. Make sure you go home and get some rest, because we have a huge weekend ahead of us in Indiana... Ce-Ce, there's a couple of reporters outside that need to speak with you. Once again, GREAT job tonight ladies..." Said Coach Law.

As Ce-Ce left out the locker room, she expected to see Zae, but she was nowhere to be found.

"Giiiiirl, you know you showed your behind on that court tonight!! Come give me a hug," said an excited Ms. Velma.

Laughing as she walked towards Ms. Velma to give her a hug, Ce-Ce said, "Aww... Thank you Na-Na! Did you see how many people were here?!"

"I heard that's going to be the norm for your games... I guess I need to make sure I make it to the games early," said Ms. Velma.

Still looking around, Ce-Ce still didn't see Zae which was odd, and it didn't sit well with her.
"You ok sweetie? What's bothering you..." Asked Ms. Velma.

Shaking her head, Ce-Ce said, "Nothing's bothering me Na-Na... I'm ok."

All Ce-Ce could think about is Zae and why she wasn't at the game... She could only hope her friend was ok.

Chapter 13

<u>Unexpected Tragedy</u>

"Congratulations to our girls basketball team with an AMAZING 88 to 61 victory over Union High School! Leading the way was freshman Cecilia Adams with 24 points and 8 assist, and senior Nychella Campbell with 21 points and 9 rebounds! Let's wish them well as they prepare to take on Indiana Institute & Technology this weekend in Hammond, Indiana," said Mr. Whittier over the school's P.A. System.

The hallways were full as everyone walked to class, and as Ce-Ce stood at her locker all she could hear is, "What's up SUPA-STAR!!"

As she turned around it was her teammate Nychella.

"You ok Ce-Ce? Why are you looking like somebody stole your dog?" Asked Nychella.

Shrugging her shoulders, Ce-Ce said, "I'm worried about my friend Zae... I haven't heard from her nor seen her since last Thursday. It's not like her to not call or not show up to our games..."

"Is there anyone you can call? Like her parents or somebody? You need to go tell somebody in the office Ce-Ce, because it could be something serious...," said Nychella.

Hearing Nychella, but at the same time looking off in deep thought, Ce-Ce replied, "Yea... But I believe she's ok."

As the school day went on, and Ce-Ce sat in her 7th hour Algebra class, someone knocked at the door, and it was Mr. Whittier.

Mr. Whittier stepped into the classroom and asked Ms. Nottingham, "May I get Cecilia Adams please? I need her to come with me."

With a look of confusion on her face, Ce-Ce didn't know what to think and wondered why Mr. Whittier was pulling her out of class.

Walking closely behind Mr. Whittier as they walked to the office, Mr. Whittier turned to Ce-Ce and said, "You can sit in my office Cecilia, I'll be with you very shortly."

"What is going on?" Ce-Ce thought to herself.

As she sat there her counselor Mrs. Jonna walked in with a Detroit Police Department Detective.

"Hi Cecilia, my name is Detective Lamont Harris, and I want to ask you some questions about your friend Zae. Is that ok?"

With a puzzled look on her face, Ce-Ce said, "Umm, I guess..., but what is going on with Zae? Is everything ok?

"We know that you two are best friends, and Mr. Whittier says he seen the two of you in the hallway crying about a week and a half ago, so I was wondering was something wrong or going on that we need to be made aware of?" Asked Detective Harris.

Ce-Ce sat up in her chair and put her head down...

"What is it Cecilia, don't be afraid to talk," said Mrs. Jonna.

Ce-Ce put her head down and took a deep breath... Looking up at Detective Harris, Ce-Ce said, "I knew I should've said something the day Mr. Whittier seen us in the hallway, but because of my loyalty to Zae, I didn't want to put her in a situation that would get her put back in placement. Zae told me how she hated going home because her father was sexually abusing her, and her alcohol and drug use was a way to take away the pain and the thought of it all... It hurt me deep because she's my friend, and I seen the pain in her eyes, and I could hear it in her voice."

The room was silent, and tears flowed down Mrs. Jonna's face as she listened to Ce-Ce recant the story Zae had told her.

Ce-Ce continued, "She told me she was tired, and she didn't want to deal with the pain anymore, and my biggest fear was Zae hurting herself or running away. When I didn't see her in school or at the games, I began to worry about her... Is she ok?"

Looking down at an envelope that he held in his hands, Detective Harris said, "I'm sorry Cecilia... Zae took her life 3 days ago, her body was found in the cellar of her home by the housekeeper. She left this letter in her room that was found by her mother, and your name is on it."

Handing Ce-Ce the envelope, Ce-Ce opened it and begun to read it out loud...

Letter to Ce-Ce: *Incest in the 21ˢᵗ Century*

"Every night I wait for my bedroom door to open, and the man I call father comes in with a Trojan; which he opens and tells me not to make a sound. I'm so broken, I'm silent as my tears hit the ground. There is no motion, I'm lifeless as he pushes inside of me. He whispers in my ear and says this is how it's supposed to be... This is my father; he wouldn't lie to me... Would he? When he's done, he tells me not to be a crybaby. He says I should be handling this better and feel loved. He says he cares about me and puts me above, but I can't shake the fact that the man married to my mother is choosing me. He tells me that this is healthy, and he's not just using me, abusing me, but I feel like I'm losing me. And yes, it hurts, but at least he's not bruising me. The man that I call daddy has stolen my virginity, and now forever is gone. Should I go tell my mom? Will she even believe me? Most days, I feel as if she doesn't even see me. What if she disowns me and calls me easy? Or what if she were to pack up and leave me? My father deceives me, he tells me that he needs me, and I need this to stop, but he's the one that feeds me..."

P.S. Ce-Ce, by the time you'll receive this letter, I'll be gone. I thank you for your genuine friendship and know that I love you.

Forever,

Zae

* * * *

As Ce-Ce finished reading the letter, she sat motionless as the paper dropped to the floor, and her heart felt like it fell into her stomach. The tears flowed down her face as thoughts ran through her head.

"I should've helped her! It's his fault!! You have to do something!" Ce-Ce yelled to Detective Harris repeatedly.

Ms. Jonna embraced Ce-Ce to console her, as she tried to find comforting words to say to her.

Mr. Whittier called Ms. Velma and asked her if she would come pick Ce-Ce up from school, and he explained to her what had happened to Zae.

Ce-Ce's mind raced as she thought about Zae, and she began to blame herself for allowing something terrible like this to happen to her.

Looking over at Mr. Whittier, Ce-Ce said, "I'm sorry Mr. Whittier... I should've said something to you about all this that day in the hallway... I won't be able to forgive myself..."

"Cecilia, it's not your fault that this happened, you were trying to be a good friend to Zae, so don't blame yourself..." said Mr. Whittier.

Shaking her head, Ce-Ce said, "This is a lot Mr. Whittier... This is really a lot."

"I understand Cecilia, that's why I called and asked Ms. Velma to come take you home for the rest of the day," said Mr. Whittier.

With a look of shock on her face, Ce-Ce said, "Home?! I don't want to go home... I can't go home. We have the Indiana Tech game coming up, and I need to be in practice. I HAVE TO be in practice Mr. Whittier."

Taking a deep sigh, Mr. Whittier looked at Ce-Ce and said, "I'm more concerned about your mental health than some basketball game Cecilia. I want to make sure you're ok, and that you're processing everything that's going on. Go home and get some rest, it's been a stressful day for you."

"I'm good Mr. Whittier... I think it's best that I stay in school and go to practice, cause that's the only stress reliever I need," said Ce-Ce.

Mr. Whittier called Ms. Velma back and told her that Ce-Ce wanted to stay in school, and if it was ok with her, he didn't mind her finishing the day.

Ms. Velma said it was fine with her, and Ce-Ce finished out the day at school.

The Perfect Stranger

As the bell sounded, Ce-Ce began gathering her books as she tried to hurry to the gym.

Ce-Ce always wanted to get extra work in before practice started, so she always finished her homework during lunch and her 7th hour class to get it out of the way.

"Hey, you need some help carrying your books to your locker?" Said an unfamiliar voice from behind her.

As Ce-Ce turned around, she became frozen as she was smitten by this handsome dark skinned 6 foot 7 inch young man named Tre Haskins.

At a loss for words, Ce-Ce could only manage to get out, "Ummm-Ummm-Ummm..."

"Don't worry, I got you... Why do you carry so many books anyway?" asked Tre.

Still somewhat at a loss for words, Ce-Ce mustard up the courage to say, "I try to get my homework done during my last class, so I can get to the gym early."

Shaking his head in agreement, Tre said, "That makes sense... I need to start doing that..."

Jokingly, Ce-Ce said, "Well, everybody doesn't want to be great..."

They both laughed as they walked out of the classroom headed to the gym. Tre Haskins was a sophomore at Kingdom Prep, whose stature was the total opposite of his personality. He was quiet and shy, which made it surprising that he even spoke to Ce-Ce. Tre was considered one of the top basketball players in his class and was highly recruited even though he was in his second year of high school. Michigan, Florida State, Missouri, Kansas, Michigan State, UConn, Gonzaga, and the list went on of all the schools that were fighting for his services.

"I'm sorry about your friend Cecilia..." Said Tre.

Shrugging her shoulders, Ce-Ce said, "Please call me Ce-Ce, and how did you know about my friend Zae...?"

Forgetting that Mr. Whittier made an announcement over the P.A. system and asked everyone to take a moment of silence.

"I remember her, she sat next to you in our 7th hour class... What's so sad, is how you're here today and gone today... How did she die? If you don't mind me asking...," said Tre.

Shaking her head, Ce-Ce said, "I rather not talk about it right now... But thanks for carrying my books... I can take them from here, I'm about to get changed so I can get some shots up..."

"Well, it was good talking to you... We have practice after y'all, so I'm sure I'll see you later... Have a great workout and practice!" Said Tre' as he walked out of the gym.

Chapter 14

The day had finally come for RJ to be inducted into the MHSCA Hall of Fame, and for his jersey to be retired at the final boys' home basketball game of the season.

"Babe, did you talk to Coach Boyd today?" Asked Honey as she flat-ironed her hair in the bathroom.

As Ray came up the stairs he said, "Yeah... I spoke to him. He wants us there 30 minutes before the game, so they can start the ceremony before tip-off. It's going to be a tough night Honey... I wonder if Bianca is going to show up."

Focusing in on her hair, Honey said, "I haven't heard anything from her..., but I did leave her a message the other day letting her know about tonight, so we'll see."

Before Honey could finish her thought, her phone rung, and it was Bianca calling.

As Honey answered, Bianca said, "Hey Mrs. Watkins, is the ceremony for RJ still happening tonight? If so, I want to know if I can ride with you all."

Honey Replied, "Of course you can ride with us sweetie... Do you need us to pick you up, or do you want to meet us here at our home? If so, please be here by 5:45.

"Thank you, Mrs. Watkins... I can be to your house at that time," said Bianca.

"Ok sweetie, that's fine... We will see you soon," replied Honey as she hung up the phone.

Reality Kicked In

As Ms. Velma walked in the house, she was surprised to find Ce-Ce there.

"You're home early today Cecilia... How are you feeling?" Asked Ms. Velma.

Laying on the couch and looking at the ceiling as if she was in deep thought, Ce-Ce said with her eyes filled with tears, "Why didn't I say anything that day Zae told me what was going on in her life? Why wasn't I strong enough to help her? WHY?!!"

Ce-Ce clutched the pillow on the couch as she cried uncontrollably.

Ms. Velma began to cry because she felt helpless, and she didn't know how to console Ce-Ce, neither did she have the words to make her feel better, so she sat on the couch and held Ce-Ce in her arms.

As they sat on the couch and Ce-Ce had settled down a bit, Ms. Velma gave her some tissue to wipe her face as she continued to rub Ce-Ce's back. Wiping her nose, Ce-Ce said, "Na-Na... It really hit me that Zae is gone... I'm sorry for breaking down like that... I'm supposed to be getting ready for the boys game tonight."

Taking her hand and raising Ce-Ce's face up to look at her eye to eye, Ms. Velma said, "There is no need for you to apologize Cecilia! I love you, and I'm here for you. If you EVER feel like leaning on me for strength, I am here for you. Do you hear me? And the last thing that should be on your mind right now is a basketball game."

Nodding her head as if to say yes, Ce-Ce began to cry again as she hugged Ms. Velma.

Ce-Ce's phone rung, as she looked down at it while wiping her face, she realized it was Nychella calling.

"Hey Nychella, what's up girl...?" Said Ce-Ce as she answered the phone.

Nychella responded, "I'm on my way to pick you up for the game, remember? Why do you sound like you're sleep or been crying? You ok? You're still going to the game, right?"

Looking over at Ms. Velma, Ce-Ce said, "Yea, I'm going to go. I need to get out of the house..."

"Ok cool, I'll be there in about twenty minutes...," said Nychella.

"I'll see you soon," replied Ce-Ce.
"Cecilia, are you sure you need to go to the basketball game? It's not a bad idea to stay in and get some rest sweetie..." Said Ms. Velma.

Taking a deep sigh, Ce-Ce said, "I'll be fine Na-Na... I think it'll be good to get out and be with my teammates at the game. They're retiring that guys jersey who played at Kingdom Prep... R.J. Watkins."

"Yes, I remember that young man... That story made national news, and it really rocked the city... I may come tonight to honor him," said Ms. Velma.

Reminiscing

"Babe, Bianca is here... We have to hurry up and go because we're running behind," said Honey as she yelled up the stairs to Ray.

Grabbing his hat and his jacket all in one motion, Ray said, "Coming down right now sweetie."

As Ray came down the stairs, he looked at Bianca, and he noticed she looked kind of nervous or as if something was troubling her.

"You good Bianca? Do you want a bottled water? Asked Ray.

Shrugging her shoulders as she walked out of the door, Bianca said, "No, I'm fine Mr. Watkins... I'm just a little nervous that's all."

As Ray got in the car and strapped on his seatbelt, he took a deep breath and said, "Yea, I think we're all a little nervous, or should I say have butterflies. It's going to be an emotional night for us all, but we have to think of the great times we had with R.J."

An emotional Honey couldn't contain herself, as she broke down and started crying uncontrollably.

Ray reached over and rubbed Honey's back, and Bianca wiped tears from her face as she cried.

Ray remained strong, but emotions twirled on the inside of him, and the pain of losing R.J. revisited him for the first time in years.

"God got us.... God got us...," said Bianca repeatedly as she sat in the back seat.

Looking in the rearview mirror at Bianca, Ray said, "Yes He does Bianca..."

Bianca went on to say, "R.J. used to say that all the time. He used to tell me, 'God got you' when I was feeling down, and I can just hear him saying that now... His voice and that saying has kept me sane all these years... I would just hear him saying, "God got you B."

Honey wiped her face and blew her nose while letting out a chuckle...

"I'm sorry guys... I just got overwhelmed with emotions, and we haven't even pulled out of the driveway yet... Bianca, I remember when I was doing my chemotherapy, I would come home and be SO exhausted." Honey laughed as she laid her head back on the headrest, and she continued saying..., "R.J. would come in my room and sit by the bed and he'll start crying because he thought I was going to die. I thought I was going to die to be honest. I would look him in the eye and tell him, "God got us, and that God had him... I miss my baby so much... It has never gotten easy."

They sat in the driveway in silence for about five minutes... "We got this, because like you said Bianca, God got US! Let's go honor R.J., so his name can live on forever," said Ray as he drove off.

Emotional Night

It was cold and windy outside, but the packed field house was buzzing with excitement. So many people came out to witness the honoring of R.J. Watkins as Coach Boyd and Kingdom Prep prepared to retire his jersey and enshrine him into the schools Hall of Fame.

"Excuse me everyone, can you all direct your attention to center court as we begin this evenings ceremony honoring arguably the greatest basketball player to ever don a Kingdom Prep Knights uniform, the late R.J. Watkins!!" Said the P.A. announcer Riley Richardson.

The audience erupted with cheers and hand claps.

Former teammates joined Coach Boyd on the court as he spoke about R.J. very vividly, and they all shed tears and laughed as they reminisced about him.

"R.J. was special in so many ways... His competitive nature, his will to be perfect at his craft, his bubbly spirit, his love for his parents and friends... All those things were unmatched. Even at his age, he seemed to be before his time... Coach! God got US!! That was R.J.'s saying, and I believe he was prophesying to us, and somehow preparing us for what NONE of us was ready for..., and that was him leaving us so soon," said Coach Boyd.

Putting his head down as if he had to gather his thoughts, Coach Boyd looked over at Ray, Honey, and Bianca and said..., "When I look at you all, I see R.J. because you three were the ones he was inseparable to. Games, events, around the city, it didn't matter R.J. was with one of you or all of you. I still pray every night for you all's strength, and I'm so happy that your bond is still tight after all these years. R.J. would be proud...

Everyone clapped as Ray, Honey, and Bianca walked to center court to join Coach Boyd.

There was not a dry eye in the building, and the energy in the gymnasium was like nothing they have ever experienced. It felt as if R.J.'s spirit swept through the fieldhouse one final time.

Coach Boyd presented them with a plaque and R.J.'s Kingdom Prep jersey in a frame, then asked Ray and Honey if they wanted to say something...

Honey looked at Ray and told him he could speak, so he took the microphone from Coach Boyd...

"First off I want to thank Kingdom Prep's administration for this beautiful ceremony honoring our son R.J., and to Coach Boyd for being a consistent friend through the years..." Looking over at R.J.'s former teammates, Ray continued and said, "To you guys, Wow... This is the true meaning of brotherhood and what love looks like. J-Mo, thank you for coming during your season, I know R.J. would be proud of you and all your accomplishments in the NBA. To everyone else, from me and my wife, we thank you from the bottom of our hearts, and want you to know that we will FOREVER be a part of the Kingdom Prep family. Love you!"

As they walked to their seats, the crowd gave them a standing ovation and the chant of "RJ-RJ-RJ!!" filled the gymnasium.

Truth Revealed

It was halftime and Kingdom Prep was winning by 16 points against a very good Jon Brown Academy of the Arts School, and Ray decided to get something to eat from the concession stand.

Ce-Ce and Nychella was standing in the hallway talking. As Ray walked by, he overheard Ce-Ce say, "We should be up by 30 points on this team, but Tre is out there playing like trash!"

Not realizing who Ce-Ce was, Ray chimed in on their conversation and said, "You know what...? You're Right. However, I believe they'll open it up in the second half..."
With a puzzled look on their faces, Ce-Ce and Nychella was trying to figure out why this stranger jumped in their conversation.

Then Nychella eyes got big and said, "Wait! You're R.J. Watkin's father! My cousin is J-Mo, who played on the team with him here..."

Ray smiled and shrugged his shoulders as if to be shy, then he said, "Yes, R.J. was my son, and J-Mo was a great player in high school, but......"

Looking down, Ray noticed a familiar face... A face that he could NEVER forget.

Ce-Ce's.

Stopping mid-sentence, Ray said..., "You're Cecilia, or Ce-Ce..., right?"

"You know him?" Asked Nychella.

With a confused look on her face, Ce-Ce said, "Umm... How do you know me...?"

Ray turned his back to Ce-Ce and pulled out his cell phone and called Honey...

"Baby, I need you and Bianca to come to the concession stand right now... You're not going to believe this," said Ray.

Not sure what was going on, Honey grabbed Bianca and they hurried to the concession stand.

"Sweety, is everything ok?" Asked a frantic Honey as she walked up to Ray. Looking at Honey, Ray turned and steadied his eyes on Ce-Ce as he nodded his head in her direction.

Honey stood motionless as she fastened her eyes on Ce-Ce... Speechless and she instantly became full of emotion.

"Mrs. Watkins, is everything ok...?" Asked Bianca as she stood close behind Honey.

Bianca looked at Ray, then she glanced at Honey to realize they were both looking in the same direction, and at the same person.

With her eyes getting big, it was as if Bianca was looking in a mirror... Then she thought to herself, "No way, it can't be..."

As everyone stood around looking at each other Mrs. Velma walked up, and she could feel the tension and awkwardness in the air.

"Hey sweetie, is everything ok?" Ms. Velma asked Ce-Ce as she looked over at Ray, Honey, and Bianca.

Clearing his throat, Ray said to Ms. Velma, "Excuse me Ma'am, are you this young ladies Mother or Grandmother?"
With a curious look on her face, Ms. Velma replied, "I'm her foster parent, why do you ask?"

"What is your name...?" Bianca asked Ce-Ce, as her eyes looked like they were filling up with tears.

"Umm Cecilia...," said a puzzled Ce-Ce....

Stepping in front of Ce-Ce, an animated Ms. Velma said, "Wait!! What is going on here? Who are you people, and why are you asking all these questions?!

With her eyes still fastened on Ce-Ce, Bianca asked, "Do you have a birth mark on your inner thigh in the shape of a pork chop?"

Shocked by what Bianca just asked her, Ce-Ce looked over at Ms. Velma and Nychella...

"How do you know that...?" Asked Ce-Ce as she started to become emotional.

Ms. Velma looked at Bianca and said, "Ok enough, what's going on here?"

Looking at Ms. Velma with tears streaming down her face, Bianca said, "My name is Bianca Elyse, and I graduated from Kingdom Prep 15 years ago... Tonight they honored my boyfriend R.J. Watkins. I was pregnant when he got murdered, and after giving birth to our daughter I left her at the hospital to be put up for adoption. I named her Cecilia Danyell Watkins. I believe this little girl is our daughter... My daughter."

For a moment, the world stood still for Ce-Ce, and the whole room began to spin...

Ms. Velma cried as she listened to Bianca's story, and she looked over to Ce-Ce and held her hand.

Ce-Ce just stood frozen and in disbelief.

To break the ice, Nychella said, "Wait, Wait, Waiiiit a minute! I know this is none of my business, but you mean to tell me that Ce-Ce is R.J. Watkins' daughter?!! Am I hearing this right? Well that explains A LOT!!

Coming out of her daze, Ce-Ce looked at Nychella and said, "What do you mean that explains a lot?"

"YOUR GAME!! The way you hoop! Girl, your pops was a LEGEND!" Nychella said with laughter and excitement.

Looking at Ms. Velma, Ray said, "Ma'am, I seen Cecilia at the park during the "Healing in the Hood" neighborhood barbeque, and I tried to find you all that day. I knew then she was my son's daughter, and my granddaughter."

"Please, call me Ms. Velma... This is just a lot to take in right now, and we're going to need some time to process everything," said Ms. Velma.
Ce-Ce walked over to Bianca and looked into her eyes... It was as if she was looking at herself, and Ce-Ce was becoming overcome with emotions.

Sobbing as she embraced Bianca, an emotional Ce-Ce screamed..., "WHY?! Why did you leave me?!!"

To Be Continued...